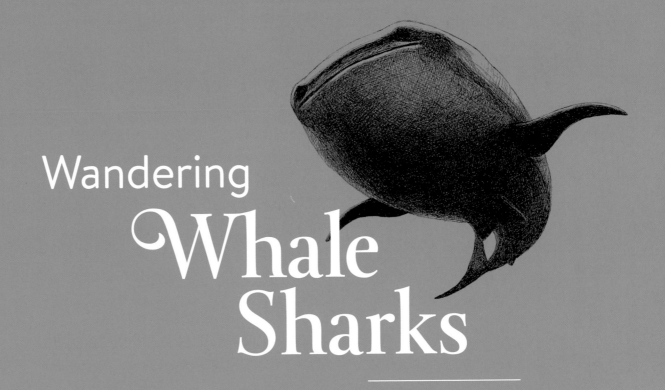

Wandering
Whale
Sharks

SUSUMU SHINGU

Owlkids Books

What human beings believe
is the surface of the sea
might just be a ceiling of air
for all the fish living below.

In the full light of the ocean,

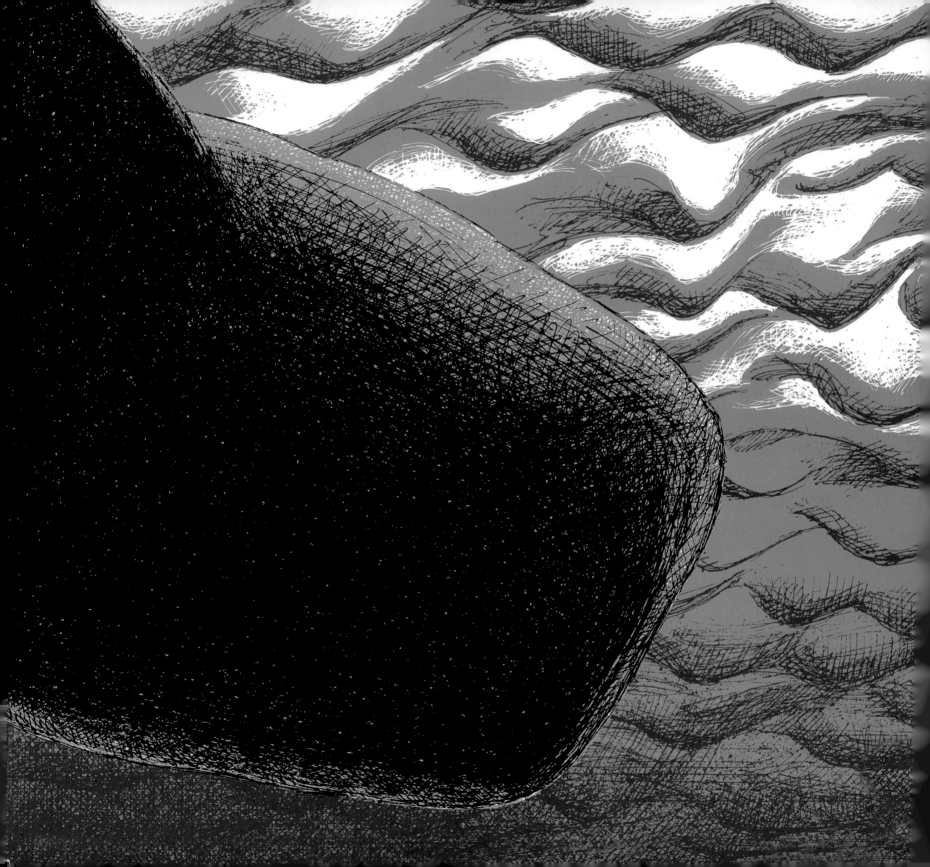

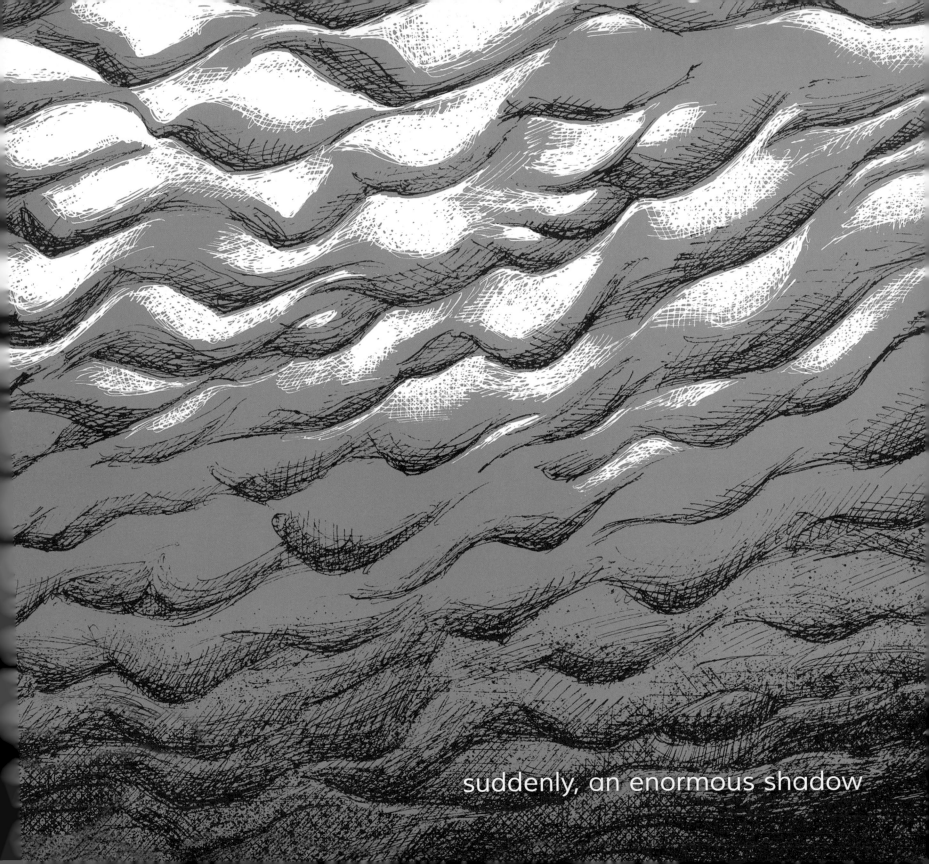

suddenly, an enormous shadow

looms,

bringing along a crowd of friends.

The fish all feel safe and secure by his side.

He is a comfortable home for suckerfish.

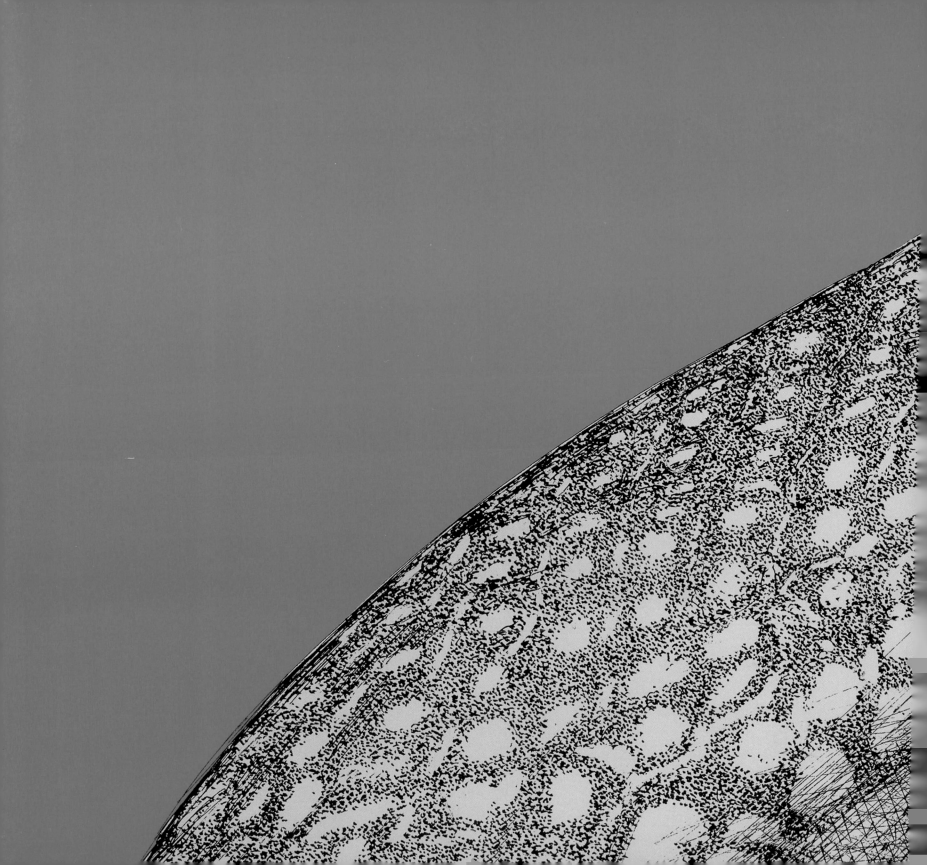

Tiny ears and gentle eyes,

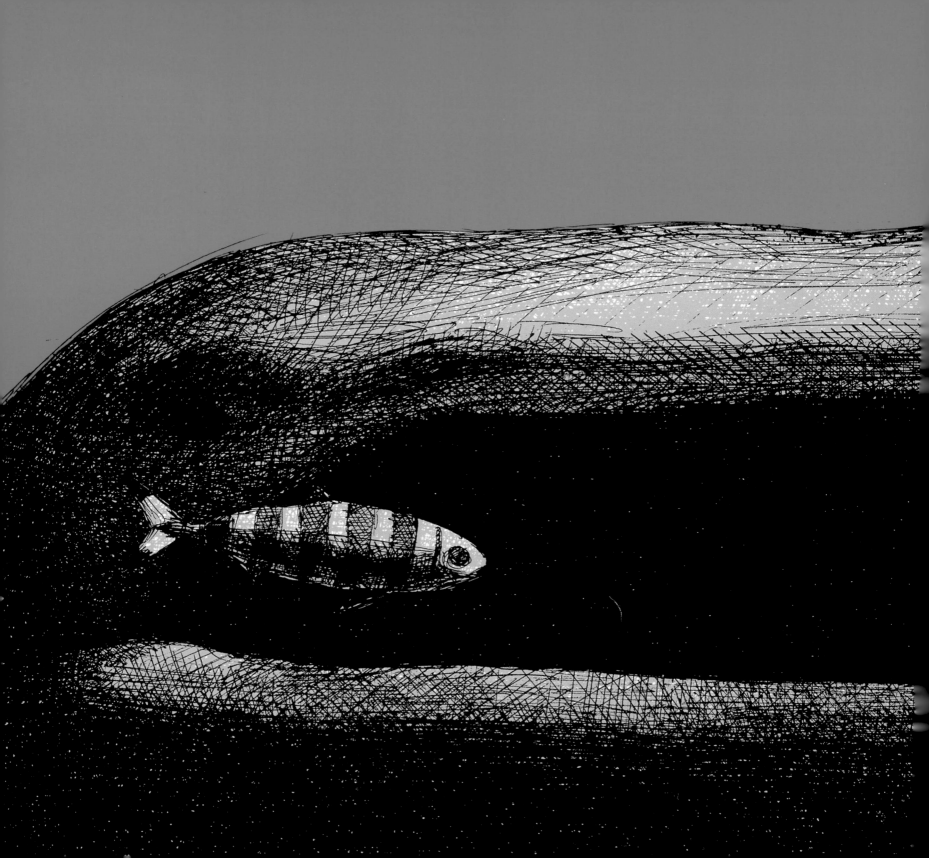

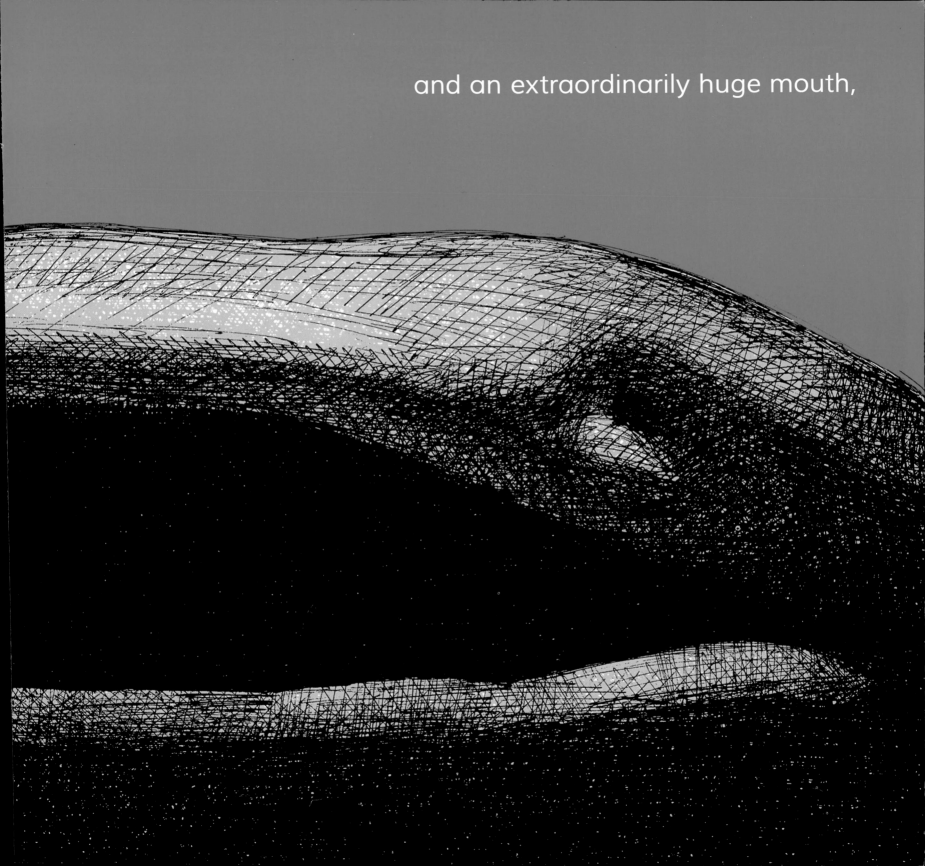

and an extraordinarily huge mouth,

swallowing tons of plankton,
shellfish, and water,

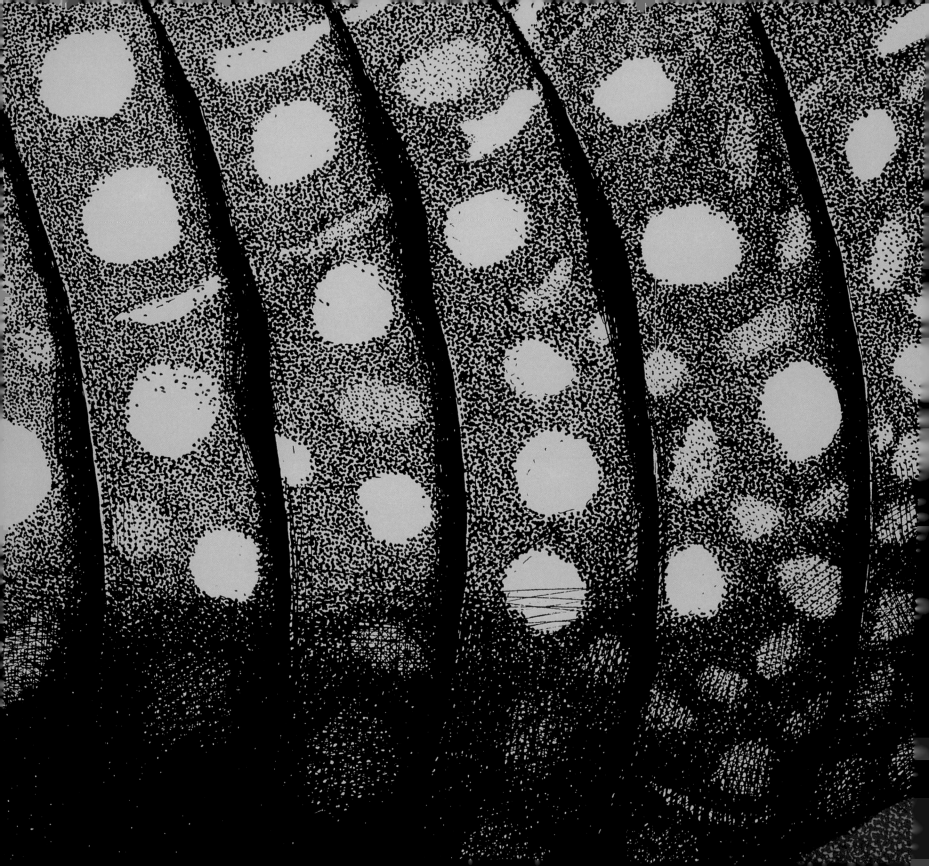

and then pushing
the water out
through his gills.

His abdomen is like a white balloon.

His back, like a mountain range, supports his great weight.

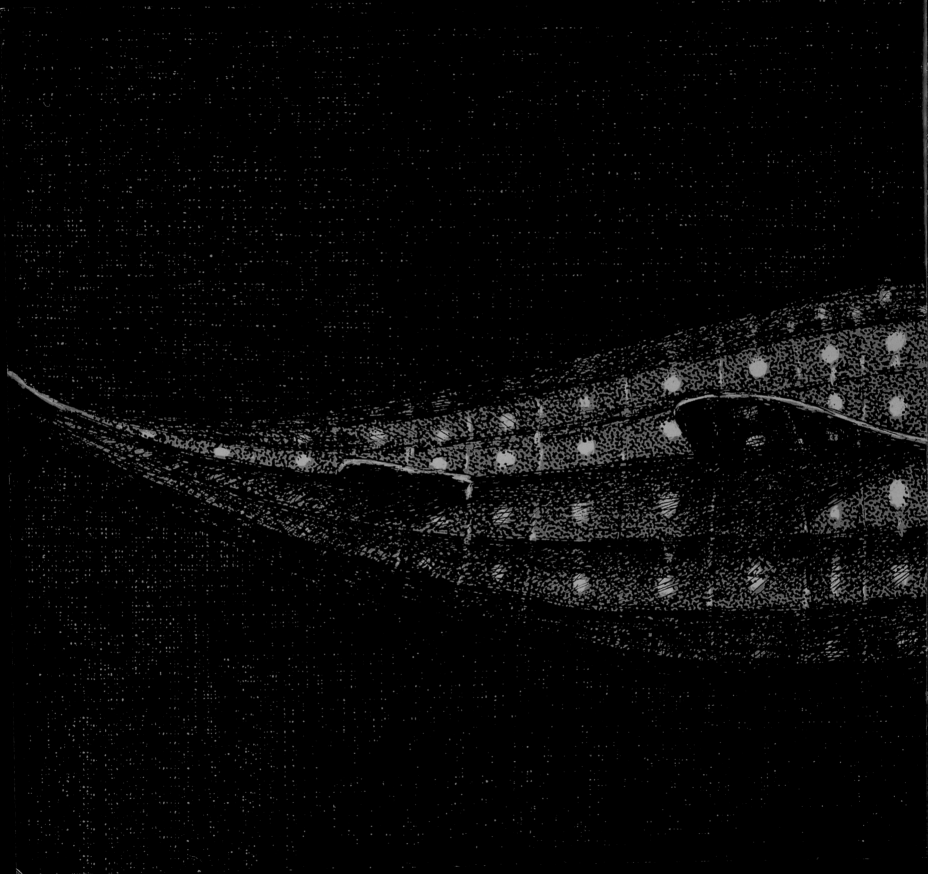

His massive body looks
speckled with snowflakes.

If you ever meet a fish
like this, don't be afraid.

He'll come along with you for a friendly swim.

Then, slowly swinging his great tail,

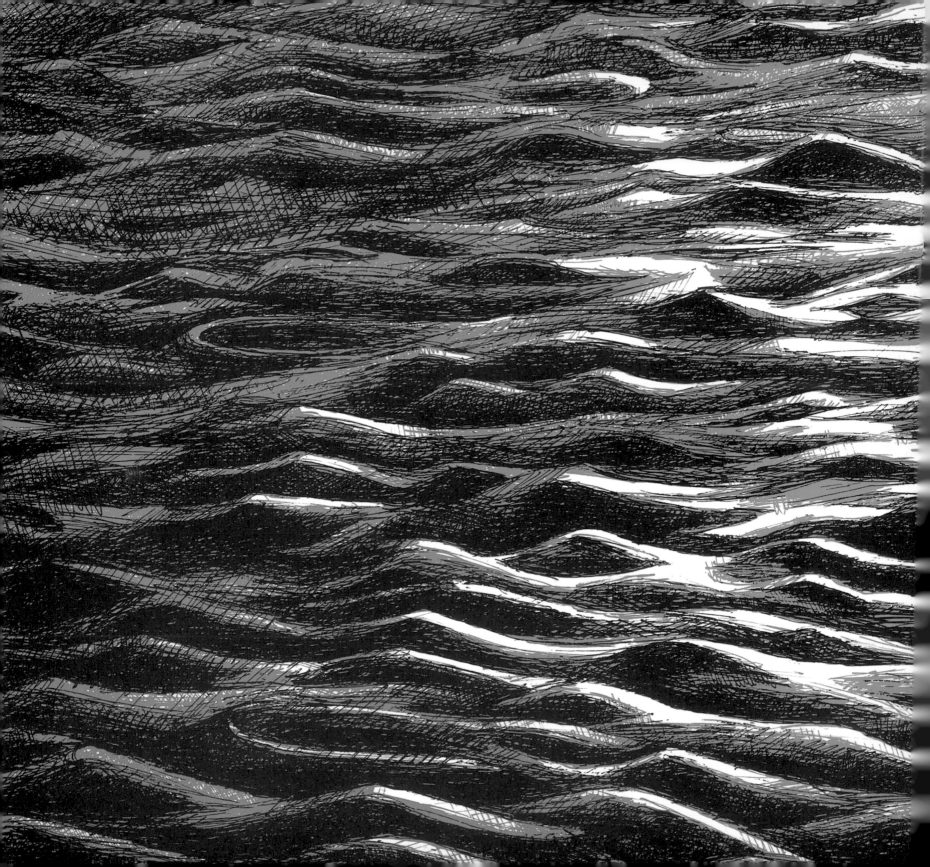

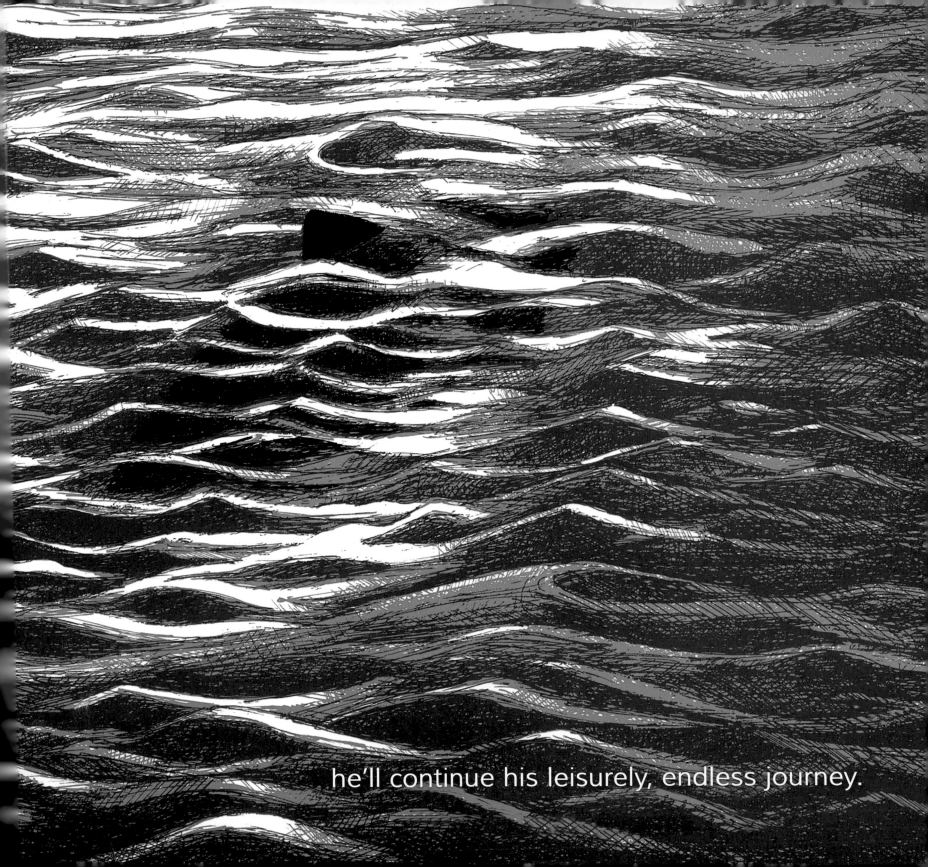

he'll continue his leisurely, endless journey.

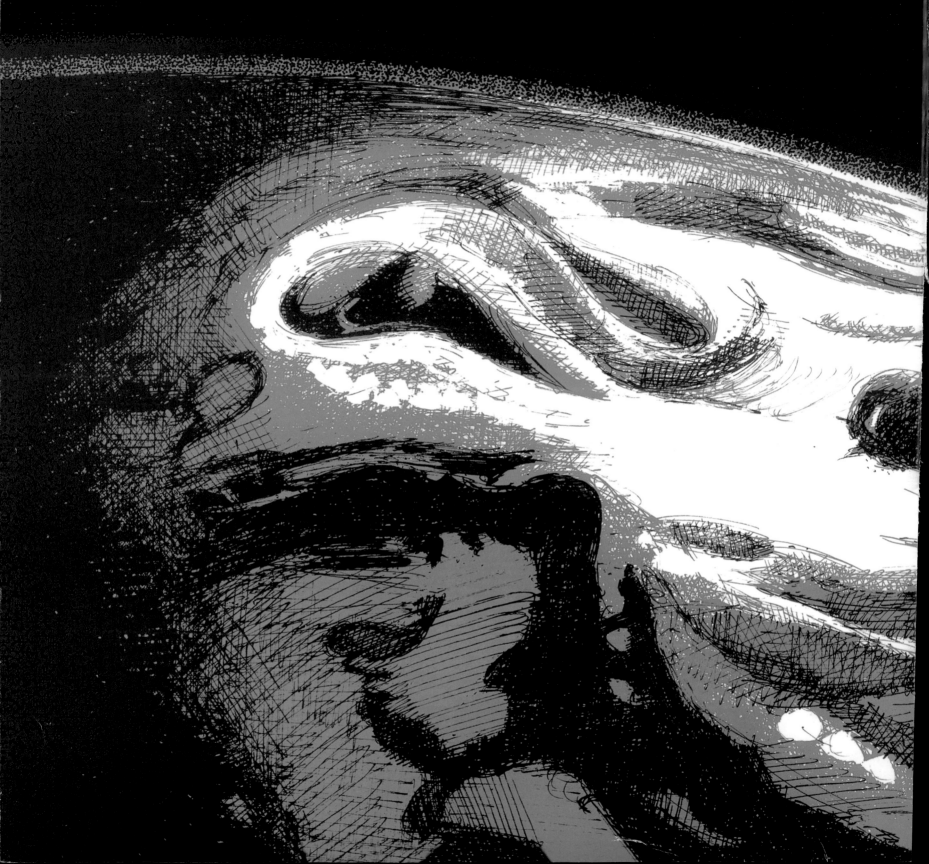

Our Earth, planet of water.

More about whale sharks

Whale sharks are the largest fish living on Earth, measuring as long as 60 feet (18 meters) and weighing as much as 44 tons (40 metric tons). Whale sharks, feeding on the plankton and small shellfish found in the huge amounts of water that pass through their gills, swim at a leisurely pace of around 2.5 miles per hour (4 kilometers per hour)—about as fast as humans can walk through water. Many fishers see them as a symbol of bounty as sardines (which also feed on plankton) and bonito (which prey on sardines) can be found trailing these enormous creatures. Whale sharks are exceedingly gentle and never attack humans. There have been reports of divers holding on to the fins of whale sharks and swimming along with them for miles. Whale sharks can be found in all tropical seas and have been spotted off the coast of several countries around the world, including South Africa, Australia, India, the Philippines, Indonesia, and Mexico. While many things about the whale shark remain to be discovered, the species is vulnerable to extinction due to human activities, such as large- and small-scale commercial fishing.

Published in North America in 2015 by Owlkids Books Inc.

First published in Japan in 1991 by FUSHOSHA Publishing Inc., Tokyo, and in 2013 by
EDUCATIONAL FOUNDATION BUNKA GAKUEN BUNKA PUBLISHING BUREAU
(Sunao Onuma, publisher), Tokyo

English translation rights arranged with EDUCATIONAL FOUNDATION BUNKA GAKUEN
BUNKA PUBLISHING BUREAU through Japan Foreign-Rights Centre

Owlkids Books acknowledges the financial support of the Canada Council for the Arts, the
Ontario Arts Council, the Government of Canada through the Canada Book Fund (CBF) and
the Government of Ontario through the Ontario Media Development Corporation's Book
Initiative for our publishing activities.

Published in Canada by
Owlkids Books Inc.
10 Lower Spadina Avenue
Toronto, ON M5V 2Z2

Published in the United States by
Owlkids Books Inc.
1700 Fourth Street
Berkeley, CA 94710

Library and Archives Canada Cataloguing in Publication

Shingu, Susumu, 1937-
[Jinbezame. English]
    Wandering whale sharks / written by Susumu Shingu; translators: Ann B. Cary and
Yasuko Shingu.

Translation of: Jinbezame.
ISBN 978-1-77147-130-5 (bound)

    1. Whale shark--Juvenile literature. I. Cary, Ann B., translator II. Shingu, Yasuko,
translator III. Title. IV. Title: Jinbezame. English.

QL638.95.R4S5513 2015   j597.34   C2014-905134-4

Library of Congress Control Number: 2014947493

Translated by: Ann B. Cary and Yasuko Shingu

Manufactured in Dongguan, China, in September 2014, by Toppan Leefung Packaging &
Printing (Dongguan) Co., Ltd.
Job #BAYDC11

A   B   C   D   E   F

Owl
kids
Publisher of Chirp, chickaDEE and OWL
www.owlkidsbooks.com